Roll
Hap
All our love,
Hunkle & Holly   xoxo
Jan. 2013

Uncle Wally's
Old Brown Shoe

Uncle Wally's
Old Brown Shoe

WALLACE EDWARDS

ORCA BOOK PUBLISHERS

Library and Archives Canada Cataloguing in Publication

Edwards, Wallace
Uncle Wally's old brown shoe / Wallace Edwards.

Issued also in electronic format.
ISBN 978-1-4598-0154-7

I. Title.
PS8559.D88U63 2012   jC813'.6   C2012-901867-8

First published in the United States, 2012
Library of Congress Control Number: 2012935414

Summary: A shoe journeys through an imaginative world to encounter a variety of intriguing animals and insects along its way. A cumulative and circular story of visual delights by Wallace Edwards.

Orca Book Publishers is dedicated to preserving the environment and has printed this book on paper certified by the Forest Stewardship Council®.

Orca Book Publishers gratefully acknowledges the support for its publishing programs provided by the following agencies: the Government of Canada through the Canada Book Fund and the Canada Council for the Arts, and the Province of British Columbia through the BC Arts Council and the Book Publishing Tax Credit.

Cover and interior artwork created using watercolor, gouache and pencil.

Cover artwork by Wallace Edwards
Design by Teresa Bubela

ORCA BOOK PUBLISHERS
PO Box 5626, STN. B
Victoria, BC Canada
V8R 6S4

ORCA BOOK PUBLISHERS
PO Box 468
Custer, WA USA
98240-0468

www.orcabook.com
Printed and bound in Canada.

15 14 13 12 • 4 3 2 1

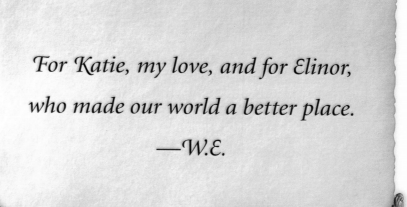

For Katie, my love, and for Elinor,

who made our world a better place.

—W.E.

This is Uncle Wally's old brown shoe.

This is the kitten
That drove around in Uncle Wally's old brown shoe.

This is the pig in the fancy hat
That tickled the kitten
That drove around in Uncle Wally's old brown shoe.

This is the frog on the handy stilts

That chased the pig

That tickled the kitten

That drove around in Uncle Wally's old brown shoe.

This is the bee with the smoochable lips

That kissed the frog

That chased the pig

That tickled the kitten

That drove around in Uncle Wally's old brown shoe.

This is the fish with the spooky mask

That startled the bee

That kissed the frog

That chased the pig

That tickled the kitten

That drove around in Uncle Wally's old brown shoe.

This is the duck with the comfortable back

That carried the fish

That startled the bee

That kissed the frog

That chased the pig

That tickled the kitten

That drove around in Uncle Wally's old brown shoe.

This is the dog with a musical flair

That played for the duck

That carried the fish

That startled the bee

That kissed the frog

That chased the pig

That tickled the kitten

That drove around in Uncle Wally's old brown shoe.

This is the plane that looped the loop

That flew over the dog

That played for the duck

That carried the fish

That startled the bee

That kissed the frog

That chased the pig

That tickled the kitten

That drove around in Uncle Wally's old brown shoe.

This is the ape on the puppet tree

That caught the plane

That flew over the dog

That played for the duck

That carried the fish

That startled the bee

That kissed the frog

That chased the pig

That tickled the kitten

That drove around in Uncle Wally's old brown shoe.

This is the moth that never sleeps

That charmed the ape

That caught the plane

That flew over the dog

That played for the duck

That carried the fish

That startled the bee

That kissed the frog

That chased the pig

That tickled the kitten

That drove around in Uncle Wally's old brown shoe.

This is the cat in the sleepy bed

That dreamed the moth

That charmed the ape

That caught the plane

That flew over the dog

That played for the duck

That carried the fish

That startled the bee

That kissed the frog

That chased the pig

That tickled the kitten

That drove around in Uncle Wally's old brown shoe.

This is the button from the cat's pajamas

That rolled away
into a dream…

And became a wheel on
Uncle Wally's old brown shoe.